Little Lora's
Animal Adventure
"I love being me!"

Dedicated
to my son, Brandon.

Once upon a time there was a little girl named Lora,
who lived with her grandmother in a
beautiful cottage near the shore of the ocean.

Lora loved her grandmother,
but sometimes she felt lonely.
Sometimes she wished she had another life.

One day while Lora was wandering along the seashore she began to wish for a different life. What would it be like to have a different life?

At that moment she saw a beautiful butterfly.
Lora watched the butterfly flying and thought,
"I wonder what it would be like to be a butterfly?
I wish I was a butterfly, I wish I was a butterfly".

Suddenly, Lora felt herself floating up and unexpectedly becoming a butterfly!

Lora was flying!
She felt wonderful soaring above the Earth!

All of a sudden, Lora saw a hawk
flying right toward her! She was afraid!

Lora thought quickly, "If I can be a butterfly,
maybe I can be a mouse and run underground."
Lora thought, "I wish I was a mouse,
I wish I was a mouse."

Lora turned into a mouse and fell to the ground.
Then she ran into a hole just as the hawk was
swooping down to get her.

Lora ran down the hole.
Her little heart was beating so fast.
"Whew that was close!" she thought.

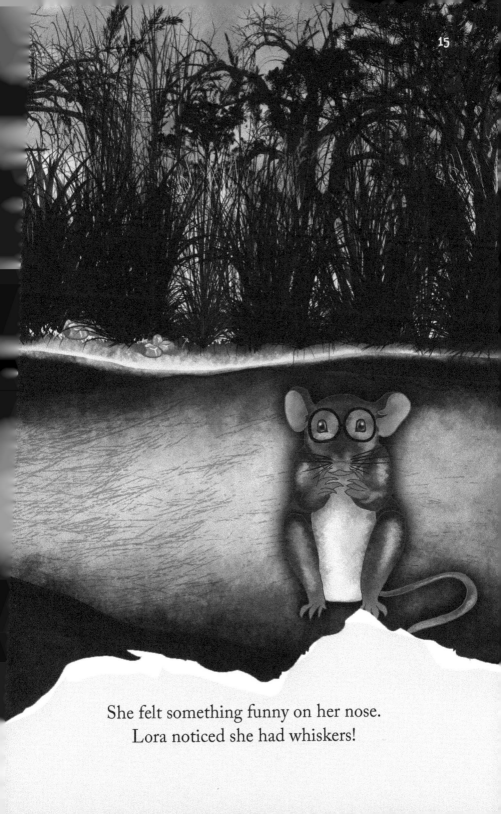

She felt something funny on her nose.
Lora noticed she had whiskers!

Curiously,
Lora scooted down the mouse hole.

Lora came to a cute little underground room,
but no one was there.
"I wonder where everybody is?" she thought.

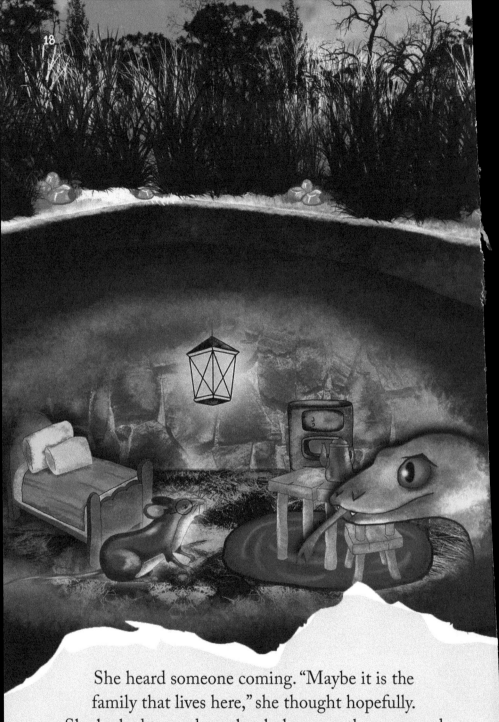

She heard someone coming. "Maybe it is the
family that lives here," she thought hopefully.
She looked toward another hole across the room and
to her surprise…she saw a giant green snake!

Lora ran toward the hole in the other direction as fast as
her four little feet could run! "What animal eats snakes?"
she asked herself. "I know! A badger!"

Just as she came to the hole's opening,
she said, "I wish I was a badger,
I wish I was a badger!"

Just as Lora jumped out of the ground and
the snake was about to bite her,
she turned into a badger.

She turned around and challenged the snake.
The frightened snake ran away!

"Whew, that was close!" she said.
"What a day!
I am tired and I am hungry."

Without hesitation, Lora started to rummage around
the ground, digging for worms.

She found a big, juicy worm, but just as she was about
to eat it, she thought,
"Yuck! I don't want to eat a worm!"

"I don't want to eat a worm, I want to eat a peanut butter and jelly sandwich, I want to go home, I want to be me, Lora. I want to be me!"

Suddenly Lora turned back into herself.
She stood up and patted her body all around.
"It's me!" she cried, "It's me!"

Lora started to run toward her
grandmother's house as fast
as her little feet could carry her!

Lora ran up the stairs and into the house.

Her grandmother was in the kitchen preparing lunch.
It was a peanut butter and jelly sandwich,
"I was wondering where you were," her grandmother said.

"Grandma, you wouldn't believe what
happened to me today!
Then Lora told her Grandmother everything
that had happened to her.

Lora hugged her grandma.
She said, "Grandma, I love our little cottage, I love peanut
butter and jelly sandwiches, and I love you!
But most of all, Grandma, I love being me!"